CONTENTS

GRACIE and The

NAME: Gracie LaRoo

TEAM: Water Sprites

CLAIM TO FAME:
Being the youngest pig to join a world-renowned synchronized swimming team!

SIGNATURE MOVE:
"When Pigs Fly" Spin

LIKES: Purple, clip-on tail bows, mud baths, newly mown hay smell

DISLIKES: Too much attention, doing laundry, scary films

QUOTE

"I just hope I can be the kind of synchronized swimmer my team needs!"

WATER SPRITES

JINI

BARB

JIA

SU

MARTHA

BRADY

SILVIA

HOG HEAVEN

Gracie LaRoo stared at the big red building.

Hog Heaven Studios.

She shivered with excitement and nerves. She was going to be in a film with Tilda Swinetune, the champion swimmer and film star!

"I wish the other Water Sprites were here with me," she whispered to herself. "Then I wouldn't be nervous at all."

A very tall sow burst through a door.

Gracie recognized Mira Patel, the most famous film director in Piggywood.

The director reached Gracie and bowed. She said, "At last you are here! I am humbled to meet the water ballet champion, Gracie LaRoo!"

Gracie couldn't speak. No one had ever bowed to her before. Especially someone famous.

Mira said, "I have watched the wonderful PigTube videos of your team. The Wiggly Piggly Pyramid! The Train of Trotters! But your spins are what dazzle me. I knew I must have you in the film. Did you receive the film script?"

Gracie nodded. "I read it on the plane," she said. "Which part is for me? I know Tilda is the Queen, but —"

Mira cut her off. "Come inside and see your stage!"

CHAPTER 2

THE SUIT

It was the biggest swimming pool Gracie had ever seen.

Mira said, "Go and peek. There is just a rehearsal going on."

Gracie climbed a ladder to see it all.

Eight pigs in bright coloured suits were in the water. Someone shouted, "One . . . two . . . three!"

One by one the swimmers dove, flipping up fishtails as their heads disappeared underwater.

Those are the merpigs! Gracie thought. Since reading the script, Gracie had hoped she would be a merpig in the film.

She also hoped her

costume would be purple.

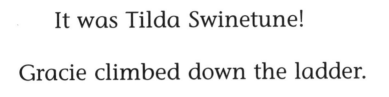

"Mira Patel, we have

to talk!" a voice called out.

It was Tilda Swinetune!

Gracie climbed down the ladder.

Tilda strode forward. She did

not look happy.

Mira trotted towards Tilda, "Gracie La Roo has arrived. Now the film will be dazzling!"

Tilda looked at Gracie. "Her? I know she's a water ballet star, but she's hardly more than a piglet!"

"But have you seen her spin?" Mira asked. "We can film her and make it look like you!"

No one will even know I'm in the film? Gracie thought unhappily. Her shoulders slumped.

Mira moved closer to Tilda.

"Just picture it: the merpig queen

is captured by pirates. But she

escapes! She celebrates by leaping

off the rocks into a circle of her

cheering merpigs. Dazzling!"

Tilda put her hooves on her hips. "I am the fastest swimmer in the world. Why isn't speed part of the story? That's dazzling!"

Mira said, "Just wait until you see her fly. Then you'll understand!"

She shouted to the film crew, "Put Gracie in the suit!"

GRACIE'S VISION

Gracie wanted to cry. "I have to

wear this?" she said and

snuffled a little.

"When you wear

that suit," Mira said,

"our special camera

films your movement.

Then we add Tilda's face and

costume when we edit the film."

She smiled. "When the audience sees the spin, they'll think she's the one doing your trick. Movie magic!"

Gracie thought, *I really wanted to be a merpig.*

The director pointed to the big pile of rocks and said, "Up you go."

Gracie looked at the very highest rock. She said, "You want me to leap from there?"

"Leap and spin," Mira said. "The flat rock on top is fake. Inside are two springs. The top of that rock will pop up and push you high into the air."

Tilda grumble-oinked. Then she sat in a chair and groinked once more.

"I'll try,"

said Gracie,

swallowing.

She climbed the

pile of rocks and

took a deep breath.

During the first

jump, the spring in

the rock pushed her too far to the

right. She splashed in the pool in

the wrong place.

The second
time, the spring
in the rock
pushed her too
far to the left.
She splashed in the
wrong place again.

Gracie climbed out of the pool
and wiped water from her eyes.
"Maybe if we –"

Tilda interrupted. "This will
never work," she said to Mira.

"It must work!" Mira said. "Her spins will make my film sensational!"

As they argued, Gracie climbed up the ladder and stared at the beautiful pool with the big pirate ship.

What if the pirates captured a merpig instead of the queen? she thought. *Then the queen could lead the pirates on a chase. That way, everyone could see how fast Tilda is!*

The angry voices below her grew even louder.

Gracie climbed down the rocks. "Please stop arguing!" she said. No one paid attention.

"I have an idea," she said a little louder.

But the argument between

Mira and Tilda got louder too.

Gracie took a big breath and

shouted, "LISTEN TO ME!"

Everyone turned in surprise.

Gracie smiled and said to the

whole crew, "I know what to do."

CHAPTER 4

DAZZLING!

The cinema was full. The lights dimmed. The screen grew bright.

Gracie wiggled with excitement. She smiled to herself in the dark cinema. She couldn't wait for her part: the smallest merpig, captured by the pirates! She concentrated on the film.

The merpigs swam around the

queen, who was Tilda Swinetune.

She wore a necklace with a huge

pearl in it.

The pirate ship came into the

picture. Gracie couldn't stop herself

from gasping. The ship looked so

much bigger on the screen.

"They want the pearl! Dive deep and swim to the caves!" yelled the queen to the merpigs.

On the screen, the camera showed a little pig in a purple mertail, flopping in a net. A pirate called out, "Too late! Give us the pearl or we'll sell your friend to a circus!"

Gracie wanted to explode with excitement. SHE was the little merpig captured. She even got to wear the purple mertail!

The queen gasped. "We must summon help from our sea friends."

An octopus appeared on the screen and threw the queen high in the air. The queen did one, two, three spins and landed on the deck of the ship.

Tilda turned in her seat and winked at Gracie. That had really been Gracie in the green suit rolling through the air. Movie magic!

After the queen freed Gracie

the merpig from the ship, she

slipped into the water to escape.

The pirates caught sight of

her. She yelled, "If you want the

pearl, try to catch me!"

The pirates tried to catch the queen, but she swam in circles around them – and led the ship right into a rock!

Crash!

The queen joined her merpigs in the moonlit water, Gracie the merpig right by her side.

THE END scrawled across the screen.

The lights went up. The audience cheered and clapped.

Gracie rose with the other

actors and took a big bow. She had

become a film star!

Tilda leaned over and whispered in Gracie's ear, "Thank you, my little flying pig."

Gracie kissed the famous actress on her cheek and then spun around three times in her purple gown.

GLOSSARY

concentrate   focus on something

dazzling   exciting!

gasping   breathe in a quick breath

grumble   complain in a low voice

humbled   feel grateful

merpig   part mermaid, part pig

nerves   being worried or anxious

scrawled   write quickly

sensational   amazing!

snuffled   sniff sadly

trotted   jog lightly

TALK ABOUT IT!

1. Can you think of a film that had special effects or had "movie magic?"

2. Why did Tilda and Mira argue?

3. What would you have done if you were in Gracie's place?

WRITE ABOUT IT!

1. Write a film starring Gracie. What would her story be?

2. Write a letter from Tilda to Mira, explaining why she wanted the film to show her speed.

3. Write an email from Gracie to the Water Sprites. What would she tell them about her experience making the film?

About the author

Marsha Qualey is the author of many books for readers young and old. Though she learned to swim when she was very young, she says she has never tried any of the moves and spins Gracie does so well.

Marsha has four grown-up children and two grandchildren. She lives in Wisconsin, USA, with her husband and their two non-swimming cats.

About the illustrator

Kristyna Litten is an award winning children's book illustrator and author. After studying illustration at Edinburgh College of Art, she now lives and works in Yorkshire in the UK, with her pet rabbit Herschel.

Kristyna would not consider herself a very good swimmer as she can only do the breaststroke, but when she was younger, she would do a tumble roll and a handstand in the shallow end of the pool.

THE WONDERFUL, THE AMAZING, THE PIG-TASTIC GRACIE LAROO!

Discover more at
www.raintree.co.uk

Find out more about Gracie and her adventures.

Follow the Water Sprites as they craft their routines.

Figure out what you would do ... if you were the awesome Gracie LaRoo!